Sparkle town Fairies

Alice
the
Amber
Fairy
and the Showstopper Spectacular

Sarah Creese * Lara Ede

make
believe
ideas

In **Sparkle Town**, for all to see,
there stood a dazzling store
full of **amber instruments**,
and with a **singing** door!

High Street

Chief Creator of things to play,
for every kind of sound,

was Alice the Amber Fairy —
the best inventor around!

Each **ten years** in Fairy Land,
a contest came to town
to choose a **fairy winner** for
the SHOWSTOPPER SPECTACULAR crown.

High Street

Dear Fairies,

We proudly present the

SHOWSTOPPER SPECTACULAR

Fairy Land's greatest musical contest!

All tuneful entries will be welcomed, but only **one** will be worthy of winning the **crown**.

Yours sincerely

Juno Jewel

SHOWSTOPPER SPECTACULAR Head Judge

It's Showstopper time!

The **Amber family** fairies had won year in, year out.

Alyssa Amber

Alfie Amber

1st

Annie Amber

Alex Amber

Astra Amber

Amelia Amber

Amy Amber

The Ambers are musical masters!

The **problem** was, poor Alice

(please promise you won't tell)

could not play **ANY** instrument

particularly well.

Too scared to tell her friends the truth
or let her family down,
Alice cried, "What can I do?
How will I win the crown?"

First she tried the **glitzaphone**
but her fingers were too slow,

Clink

Clunk

Me-oww!

Toot

then she tried the **sparklehorn**
but her "toots" came out too low.

The **glitter chimes** all clashed together,

CLASH

CLANG

the bells went

ding,

dong,

wrong!

Rinnnnng

Her **drumming** sounded too offbeat and the cymbals rang too long!

So Alice **worked** all through the night,
inventing **more** and **more**
until she created something
unlike anything seen before...

High Street

She took a breath, then blew inside
and **without touching a key**,

the instrument played **ON ITS OWN**,

and was **TUNEFUL** as can be!

Alice practised "**playing**" to make her act look true until she was finally ready for her **Showstopper** debut.

As Alice watched each one perform
and play their part with pride,
she felt **guilty** about tricking them
and knew she could not lie.

Alice was called to start her piece,
and the crowd let out a cheer
(for Alice's music was the act
they most wanted to hear).

"Umm...before I start," said Alice,
"there's something I **must** say.
I'm not a good musician;
in truth, I **cannot play**.

I **created** this machine
to cover up who I am.
This instrument plays on its own;
I'm really just a **sham**."

The fairies **gasped** together. They hadn't expected that!
As Alice began to tremble, Esme appeared from the back.

Well, that was a surprise.

Oh, my!

She smiled and hugged poor Alice. "Don't feel blue," she said. "You may not be a **Showstopper**, but you're our **inventor** instead."

Alice did not play her piece,
and the **Showstopper** was won
by the most deserving fairy,
chosen by everyone.

Hurrah!

Go on, Alice!

At the **afterparty** later,
the fairies all agreed:
there was one thing that the party
did really, truly need.

They cried to Alice all at once,
"We want to hear you play!"
So Alice grinned and took a breath
and without further delay . . .

it went...

Toot-Toot, la-de-da,

Though the special instrument
was **famous** near and far,

Alice learnt that **best** of all
is being **who you are!**